Discovery on
Blackbird Island

The Gun Lake Adventure Series
Book 3

by Johnnie Tuitel and Sharon Lamson

CEDAR TREE PUBLISHING

DISCOVERY ON BLACKBIRD ISLAND
Copyright 2000 by Johnnie Tuitel and Sharon E. Lamson

Published by Cedar Tree Publishing
1916 Breton Rd. SE
Grand Rapids, MI 49506
1-888-302-7463 (toll free)

Second Printing
Cover and Illustration: Dan Sharp

Library of Congress Catalog-in-Publication Data
Lamson, Sharon E. 1948–
Tuitel, Johnnie, 1963–
Discovery on Blackbird Island/Johnnie Tuitel and Sharon Lamson

cm.—(The Gun Lake Adventure Series)

Summary: An end-of-the-summer outing leads to an unusual discovery. "Wild animals" on the unpopulated Blackbird Island? The Gun Lake kids are hot on the trail to finding out how the animals got there and why. New dangers are faced and new friendships formed.

ISBN 0-9658075-2-5

[1. Adventure stories—Fiction 2. Mystery and detective stories—Fiction 3. Physically Handicapped—Children—Fiction 4. Michigan—Fiction]

I. Title   II. Series: Lamson, Sharon E., 1948–, Tuitel, Johnnie, 1963–

(The Gun Lake Adventure Series)

99-076760

DEDICATION

To my children Kim, Heather, Brittany, Josh and Robyn. And to my grandchildren George, Johnathon, Veronica, Jazzmond and my adopted grandchildren Maxi Jean and Paradise. Children are indeed a blessing from God—and I have been truly blessed.

—Sharon E. Lamson

To my good friend Dani and the Bellwether Foundation for helping stray animals find new homes.

To Paws With A Cause for their wonderful gift of Steamer.

And to Steamer.

—Johnnie Tuitel

Acknowledgment

Many thanks to Kellie Grant, Joe Gutowski, John Kartes and Brittany Lamson who helped shape this book through their very perceptive (and sometimes painful) edits. (Smile!)

Table of Contents

CHAPTER 1

Tubing on Gun Lake

"Faster!" Johnnie Jacobson yelled. "Go faster!"

Mr. Randall glanced at his son Danny, who watched his friend bounce and splash across Gun Lake on a large, yellow speed tube being pulled behind the Randalls' ski boat. The speed tube was designed with netting in the bottom of the hole that the tube formed. A harness encircled the tube and was fastened to the pull rope. Johnnie lay across the tube on his stomach and hung onto the handles attached to both sides of the tube. Using his forearms and elbows, Johnnie could steer. When a wake rushed toward him, he lifted the front end of the tube by pulling back on the handles and pressing his knees into the netting.

Johnnie gripped the handles tightly and yelled, "Can't you go any faster?"

Danny shook his head and grinned. "You're nuts!" he yelled back at his friend.

Johnnie smiled broadly and nodded his head in agreement. Mr. Randall eased the throttle forward, and the tube carrying Johnnie lifted higher out of the water. He leaned from side to side as the boat turned and the waves, caused by other motorboats on the lake, rolled toward him.

Through the spray of water, 11-year-old Johnnie could see his friends Danny and Katy Randall, Robyn Anderson and Travis Hughes squinting into the wind as Mr. Randall made a large circle around the lake. He knew there was no other place on earth he would rather be.

Usually, the kids' younger friends — Nick Tysman and Joey Thomas — would be there, screaming for Mr. Randall to go faster, but they were away on separate last-of-the-summer vacations. Johnnie missed their laughter.

It had been only a few months since Johnnie and his family made the move to Gun Lake, Michigan from California. Although Johnnie had cerebral palsy and needed to use a wheelchair to get around, he had learned how to ski at a very young age. A special water ski called a "kanski" had been developed for people with physical disabilities. It was like one extra-large ski with a special seat bolted to the middle, and a place near the front where the ski rope could be attached. Johnnie remembered his first skiing lesson out on the glassy waters of Lake Tahoe. He had been excited and scared all at the same time. With his father's reassurance, Johnnie sat in the ski, grabbed hold of the ski rope and held his breath as the boat took off.

Johnnie's older brother had skied alongside him, shouting out instructions: "Lean left! Lean right! Hang on!"

It wasn't long before Johnnie had the art of skiing—and falling—down pat. Shortly after, he and his brother came up with the idea of tubing. "It's the same idea as sitting in a kanski," Johnnie said. "Plus then I can flip out of it easier," he added with a grin.

Now, in Michigan, there were plenty of opportunities for water sports. Johnnie chuckled as he remembered the look on Travis' face when Johnnie suggested they all end the summer with a big water skiing party. "What are you going to do," Travis had asked, "ski on your stomach?"

"Just watch me," Johnnie replied.

Eleven-year-old Travis was the school athlete. Johnnie didn't think there was *any* sport Travis wasn't good at. Proving to Travis that he was good at water sports was important to Johnnie.

But Mr. Randall wasn't too sure about taking Johnnie out on the lake in a speed tube. One call to Johnnie's father reassured him, however. "It sounds like the ski party will be a lot of fun," Mr. Jacobson had said. "Don't worry about Johnnie. He's a great tuber—and he's a good swimmer too."

With Johnnie's life jacket securely fastened, Mr. Randall sped around the lake as fast as he dared.

"Driftwood!" Travis yelled, pointing just ahead of them. Mr. Randall swerved sharply to the left to miss it. The unexpected swing of the boat caught Johnnie leaning the wrong way in the tube. Out he popped from the speed tube. He immediately let go of the handles and was airborne.

He flew a few feet in the air, arms and legs extended, and then landed with a tremendous splash in the water. Just as fast as he plunged beneath the water, he bobbed to the surface again.

As Mr. Randall quickly circled the boat back to where Johnnie was splashing about, Danny held up a special flag to indicate a skier (or in this case, a tuber) was in the water. It was a warning signal to other boaters in the area to be extra careful.

"What's he yelling?" Robyn asked, brushing strands of her dark-brown hair from her eyes.

"He's laughing," Danny replied. "Looks like he's saying, 'Wipe out!'"

When the boat pulled up alongside Johnnie, Danny asked, "Hey, are you okay?"

"I'm way okay!" Johnnie said with a grin. "That was so awesome!"

"Well give me your hand and I'll help you in," Danny said. The sun glistened off Danny's sun-bleached hair.

"I've got a better idea," Johnnie replied. "It's only a short way to Blackbird Island, just over there." He pointed toward the small, wooded island. "Let's swim to shore!"

Danny gave his dad an "is-it-okay" look. Mr. Randall gauged the distance between where they were and the shoreline and decided it was a safe enough distance. "Sure, go ahead!"

"Hey! I've got an idea," said Danny. "Why don't I go back to Gun Lake with my dad? I'll pick up our picnic stuff and meet you back at the island. I can use our small motorboat. Then we can do some island exploring before we head back."

"Sounds like fun to me!" Katy said. "How about it, Dad? Can we? Please?" Katy, though only eight years old, was a strong swimmer.

Mr. Randall chuckled. "I guess that will be fine as long as you're back before dark—and as long as you don't go to any of the other islands." Then to Danny he said, "Before we head back, why don't you and I go trolling for driftwood? I know Johnnie thought that little incident was funny but it sure scared the heck out of me!"

Johnnie watched as, one by one, all the kids except Danny jumped into the cool water. While Johnnie could swim well, the life jacket made his progress slow. Pretty soon, Katy, Robyn and Travis were far ahead of their friend.

"Hey! Wait up!" Johnnie yelled.

"You guys go ahead," Robyn said. "I'll go back and swim in with Johnnie."

As Katy and Travis swam the last few feet to shore, Robyn trod water and waited for Johnnie to catch up.

"That was totally awesome!" Johnnie said when he finally reached Robyn. "I think wiping out is the most fun part of tubing or skiing."

"Well, you sure looked funny flying through the air. You looked like a human Frisbee going straight up and then falling straight down."

"Well, at least this time I didn't lose my swimming trunks. I usually do, you know! This has been the best summer I've ever had!" Johnnie said. "When I first moved here from California, I thought it would be boring."

Robyn laughed. "Well, with you around, it seems we've had our share of adventures this summer. Even though it's been fun, I'm kind of glad school will be starting soon."

"That ought to be an adventure all in itself," Johnnie said.

It wasn't long before Robyn and Johnnie joined the others on the white, sandy beach of Blackbird Island. Johnnie pulled himself up onto the beach and lay there catching his breath.

Behind them, willowy blades of dune grass grew out of

the sandy soil. Beyond the gentle slopes, bushes and trees thickly blanketed the island. Besides birds, insects and an occasional turtle, nothing lived there.

"This place is so peaceful," Katy said as she sat on the sand gazing at the blue sky. A gentle breeze tousled her blonde hair. "I wish I could live here."

"Me too!" Robyn agreed. "But not in a regular house— maybe a tree house or something."

Travis rolled his eyes. "Yeah, right! The first time a storm would come whipping in off Lake Michigan and head toward Gun Lake, you guys would be screaming and wanting to come home."

"Oh, whatever," Robyn snapped back. Then to avoid an argument, she said, "While we're here and waiting for Danny to come back, why don't we do some exploring? Maybe we'll find an end-of-the-summer adventure right here on Blackbird Island!"

CHAPTER 2

Exploring Blackbird Island

Exploring Blackbird Island by pulling himself through the sand and woods wasn't exactly what Johnnie had in mind. He watched as Katy, Robyn and Travis scurried off into the woods.

"Fine!" he yelled. "Go exploring. Leave me here by myself. At least I won't get poison ivy!"

He watched Katy stop and slowly turn around. She walked back to where Johnnie sat. "Okay, you're right," she said. "Come on, you guys," she yelled toward Travis and Robyn. "Let's just sit here with Johnnie and watch the water."

"What?!" Travis yelled back. "There's no way—"

"Oh, yes there is," Robyn interrupted. She grabbed Travis' arm firmly and pulled him back to the beach.

"Okay, Johnnie. We're all here," Katy said as she plopped down on the warm sandy beach.

For a long while, no one said anything. The four of them sat staring out at the lake.

"I can't stand it!" Johnnie's voice shattered the silence.

"Go exploring already! You guys are driving me nuts."

Katy looked at Johnnie. "Why? What are we doing that's driving you nuts?"

"You're thinking about exploring the woods so loudly that I can hear it in *my* mind," he said with a grin.

"Maybe that's your conscience speaking," Travis said. He got up and brushed the sand from his swimming trunks.

Robyn and Katy stared at Travis but remained seated.

"What?" Travis said. "The man said we were driving him nuts. He said to go exploring. He said he could read our minds! I'm out of here!" He tromped off toward the trees.

"Well?" Johnnie said. "Is Travis the only one who understands English? Or are you two glued to the sand?"

Robyn chuckled. "Okay. We're going—if you're sure it's all right."

Johnnie smiled. "I'm sure! I think I'll just lie here, soak up some rays, and catch a few Zs—if you know what I mean. And, if you find anything really cool, be sure to wake me up!"

Katy and Robyn looked at each other and smiled. "You'll be the first to know if anything cool turns up on this island," Katy said.

"Wait a minute," Robyn said. "I thought I heard something."

"What? An adventure already?" Johnnie said and started to laugh.

"Shhhh," Robyn whispered. "Listen! Did you hear that?"

"Sounded like a sea gull somewhere," Katy said.

The three friends became very still and strained to hear the sound again. Just then, Travis crunched his way out of the woods. "Didn't you say this island was uninhabited except for birds?" he asked.

"*That's* what I've been told," Katy answered.

"Well, just a minute ago, I could have sworn I heard a kitten meowing," Travis said.

"That's what I heard," Robyn said. "I didn't think it sounded like a sea gull. But a kitten? How in the world would a kitten get on this island? Cats hate water!"

"Oh, it *couldn't* have been a kitten," Katy said. "It must have been something else."

"Well, I intend to find out," Robyn said. "Come on, you two, let's find out where that sound came from. Johnnie, as soon as Danny gets back, let him know where we are. And if *you* hear any meowing or see anything furry running around, give a yell and we'll come back."

"No problem!" Johnnie said. He watched his friends head back into the woods. Then he turned his focus back to the lake and waited for Danny to get back with the motorboat. A tingling of excitement broadcast its way through Johnnie's body.

CHAPTER 3

Discovery on Blackbird Island

Johnnie scooted toward the edge of the water and let the waves gently wash over his feet. High overhead, the seagulls squawked and screeched as they scanned the lake for fish. Johnnie knew that once Danny arrived with their lunches, the gulls would assume they were invited to the picnic and would begin bumping and pushing each other to be first in line for whatever handouts the kids would offer.

The hot August sun was nearly directly overhead, and the humid summer air stirred lazily with the ever-present lake breeze. Ski boats, motorboats and jet skis buzzed across the lake, and swimmers dotted the water near the main shoreline.

Johnnie could hear the muffled voices of Robyn, Katy and Travis as they trampled their way through the tangled bushes and trees. As he watched the horizon for Danny to return in the small motorboat, he kept alert for unusual animal sounds—or unusual sounds of any kind. Once or twice, he could hear the distinct calls of cardinals, robins and crows. A couple times he heard the raspy quack of a pair of ducks as they flew over the lake. But he heard nothing out of the ordinary.

Still, he had a feeling that something exciting was about to happen. "Maybe the sound they heard was really a trap!" he said to a passing seagull. He glanced back at the woods. "If I wanted to lure someone to my hiding place, I might make some weird sounds—but not too weird. I wouldn't want to scare them away."

Johnnie lay back on the warm sand and closed his eyes. His imagination began forming an action-packed adventure. He could picture his friends creeping slowly toward the center of the island. Suddenly, Robyn would say, "There! I heard it again. I think it's coming from behind those oak trees." Then they would slash their way through vines and huge, "menacing" weeds.

Travis would push the girls aside as he charged forward, despite their warnings. Suddenly, the earth would give way and Travis would fall into a deep pit. A hairy pair of hands would swoop down from the overhead branches and grab Katy, whisking her back into the trees before she could even scream. And then there would be Robyn, who would start to cry.

In Johnnie's mind he could picture himself in a power-driven "hover" chair hacking his way through the jungle with his machete—its long, sharp blade slicing through branch limbs and vines as though they were butter. "I'll rescue you," he'd yell. Using his strong arms, he'd attach a vine to his hover chair and lower the green "rope" into the pit. Travis would climb to safety.

Then on to save Katy from the monstrous gorilla-like creature. It would travel fast, but Johnnie would be faster. Closing in, Johnnie would reach out and grab the beast's arm, wrestling it to the ground. It would lose its grip on Katy—but not to worry. Johnnie would catch her and put her safely on the ground before doing battle with this ancient monster.

But suddenly, the monster did a very strange thing. It began licking Johnnie's face. "Hey!" Johnnie yelled. "That's not the way this is supposed to end. Cut it out!"

Suddenly, Johnnie awoke. He was still lying on his back on the beach—the form of a furry beast blocking his view of the sun.

Startled, Johnnie rolled over and gave a yell. "Get away from me!"

The furry creature bounded away from Johnnie and sat looking at him from a safe distance. Johnnie rolled onto his stomach and looked up. He couldn't believe his eyes.

There, not five feet from him, sat a little golden retriever puppy, its head cocked to one side and its little tail acting like a windshield wiper in the sand. When Johnnie rolled onto his back and sat up, the puppy darted back toward the woods.

"Hey! Wait a minute," Johnnie called out, trying to sound friendly. "I'm sorry, fella, I didn't mean to scare you." He patted the sand and tried to coax the puppy to come back to him but the animal wouldn't budge.

Frustrated, Johnnie lay back down on the sand and tried to think of a way to get the puppy to come to him. While he lay there, he felt a cold, wet nose nudge him. Johnnie slowly turned his head and eyed his little visitor. He put out his hand and let the puppy smell it, and then he began petting the animal. His newfound friend lost no time in giving Johnnie a thorough puppy-tongue welcome.

Johnnie sat up and laughed as the puppy romped around in the sand, yipping and wagging his tail. "Wait till my friends see you!" he said. "They thought you were meowing!"

"It wasn't the dog that was meowing!" Robyn's voice startled Johnnie and he looked behind him. There was Robyn carrying—or trying to carry—a tiny calico kitten. The kitten was obviously nervous with the puppy romping about, but Robyn was able to keep hold of it.

"You wouldn't believe what I had to go through to get

this kitten. I never knew a cat could squeeze itself into such small openings."

A kitten? A puppy? Johnnie stared in amazement at the two small creatures. Travis and Katy arrived on the scene just as the persistent sound of a motorboat came closer and closer.

"Hey! There's Danny!" Travis said. "I'll help him beach the boat."

Before long, Danny and Travis came running down the beach carrying lunch supplies and drinks. "Travis tells me you guys have found some wild game!"

He stopped dead in his tracks and stared unbelievingly at the reddish-gold ball of fur darting around Johnnie and climbing into his lap. "A puppy!" he gasped.

"Yes, and look at my 'wild game,'" Robyn said. She held the orange, black and white kitten so Danny could see it.

"How on earth did these animals get here?" Danny asked. "Where did you find them?"

"Well, I thought I heard a mewing sound coming from the woods," Robyn said. "Katy and I split up and tried to pinpoint where the sound was coming from. I stood as still as I could and just listened. It seemed to be coming from the bushes just a few feet away from me. I crept as quietly as I could toward the sound and then I saw a streak of orange and black race from the bushes toward a fallen tree. I knew right then and there it was a kitten. It backed its way into a hollowed-out log, and it took a lot of stretching and reaching before I could get it out of there."

"Just about then, I found Robyn and helped her calm down the kitten," Katy added.

"What about you, Johnnie? Where did you find that puppy?" Danny asked.

"It found me! I was just lying here dreaming, and the next thing I knew, this puppy was here!"

"Hmm," Travis interrupted. "A puppy and a kitten—on an island. This just doesn't make sense. Obviously someone had to bring them here—but why? They're both young and kind of cool looking. Surely someone could have found homes for them rather than just dumping them off."

"Not necessarily," Johnnie said. "People drop off animals in the country all the time. They think that cats and dogs can hunt for their own food and take care of themselves. But most of the time, these animals just die. I remember my dad telling me that there is such an overpopulation of dogs and cats that it's getting harder and harder to find good homes for kittens and puppies."

"Well, we just can't leave them here," Katy said, petting the kitten. "They're too little to care for themselves. Let's hurry up and eat our lunches and then head back home. We can wrap them in our towels so they won't get scared and jump off the boat."

"Good idea," Johnnie said. "And then let's try to figure out why these animals were brought here in the first place!"

CHAPTER 4

Steamer and Perelandra

Johnnie and Travis wrapped a towel around the excited puppy. Johnnie pulled himself into the beached motorboat while Danny held it steady. Travis handed the puppy to Johnnie and then helped Robyn wrap the kitten in another towel.

"This is like trying to wrap a cactus," Travis complained. The kitten was frightened and desperately tried to jump out of Robyn's arms. Tiny claws and teeth battled the towel as Robyn struggled to keep the kitten under control. Finally, with Katy's help, the kitten was securely bundled.

"You don't think it will suffocate in that towel, do you?" Katy asked.

"Once we're in the boat, I'll loosen the towel a bit to let in some air," Robyn replied.

Travis and Danny pushed the motorboat into the water. Katy scrambled in first and took the kitten from Robyn while she climbed in. With everyone aboard, Danny said, "Better hold on tightly to those animals while I start the motor."

Sure enough, the moment the motor roared to life, the startled puppy and kitten tried to get away. Johnnie and Robyn spoke softly to the frightened animals and tried to reassure them. The boat pulled slowly away from the island and headed back to the town of Gun Lake.

The kitten finally settled down and Robyn relaxed her grip slightly. The puppy, however, did not like being held in a blanket and wriggled around like a bowl of jello. Out popped the puppy's head from the towel.

"Okay," Johnnie said. "I guess you can look around."

But the sight of the water only made the puppy more nervous. When Johnnie tried to hold him tighter, the puppy let out a yelp. "Sorry, pup!" Johnnie said as he eased his hold.

The puppy felt Johnnie's grip relax and took that moment to totally free himself from the towel. In an instant, the puppy scurried toward the side of the boat and lost its balance.

"Cut the motor!" Johnnie yelled. "The puppy fell in the lake."

Danny maneuvered the motorboat around so that the propeller was facing the opposite direction of the puppy. He shut off the engine. By instinct, the puppy began "dog-paddling" toward the shore.

"Wow!" Travis said. "Look at him go."

"He reminds me of a little steam engine," Johnnie said. "But I don't think he's going to make it to shore."

"Here, Katy, you take over driving the boat and I'll go fetch the dog," Danny said. "My life jacket will help me stay afloat while I bring him back."

In an instant Danny was in the water, swimming toward the now-struggling puppy. "Come on, fella," Danny said as he approached the tired animal. "I won't hurt you. Let's get back into the boat."

The puppy seemed to sense that Danny was there to help. He offered no resistance when Danny placed his arm around his body to begin hauling him back toward the boat.

"Here, take him," Danny said, as he held the puppy up toward the side of the boat. Johnnie reached down and carefully brought the puppy inside to safety. He gently began drying the soggy dog with the towel. "Man, you started out great—but you just ran out of steam! Hey! I think I'll call you 'Steamer!'"

The puppy looked up at Johnnie and gave him a quick little lick, then nestled himself in Johnnie's arms.

"Looks like he approves of his new name!" Katy said. "But are you sure your parents are going to let you keep him?"

He gave Katy a sly look. "I'm sure!" he said. "I've always wanted a dog, but with moving and everything we just never got one. This puppy found me! And he's got nowhere else to go. My parents are pretty cool. They'll let me keep him." But inside, Johnnie was a little worried.

With Danny back in the boat, the kids and their newfound animal friends headed back to Gun Lake. The kitten was gently purring as it rested peacefully in Robyn's lap. Steamer closed his eyes and slept for the rest of the short journey.

At the dock, everyone scrambled out of the boat. Johnnie's wheelchair was bike-locked to the bicycle rack at the end of the dock. Danny unlocked it and brought it onto the wooden walkway. He waited until Johnnie was able to hoist himself out of the boat and into the chair. Travis handed him the sleepy puppy. Danny looked at the puppy curled in Johnnie's lap. "Why don't you hang onto Steamer and let me push you home," he offered.

Johnnie smiled. "Thanks!" he said. "That would sure help."

Johnnie, Travis and Danny lost no time in getting to Johnnie's house. Mrs. Jacobson was outside tending to her herb garden when she saw the boys coming.

"Mom!" Johnnie yelled. "Guess what we found on Blackbird Island!"

The puppy, upon seeing Mrs. Jacobson, jumped out

of Johnnie's arms and ran straight over to where she was kneeling. He jumped around, excitedly wagging his tail. His little face broke into a puppy smile as he climbed right up into her lap.

Mrs. Jacobson laughed. "Um," she said, "let me guess. You found a puppy!"

"Well, actually, he found me," Johnnie said. And then he told her the whole story. "Can we keep him, Mom? Please?"

"Well, I don't know," Mrs. Jacobson began. "We'll need to ask your father about this when he gets home from work. After all, it is a family decision, as we'll all have to help take care of him. But in the meantime, I'll go to the store and get some puppy food for him. He looks hungry."

Johnnie smiled. He had a strong feeling that his dad, who loved dogs, would give the final okay. "Steamer," Johnnie whispered to himself, "I think you've found yourself a new home."

Meanwhile, Robyn and Katy walked to Robyn's house—the kitten now stirring and anxious to look around.

"Do you think your parents will let you keep her?" Katy asked. "I mean, you guys already have a dog, two birds and two cats."

Robyn laughed. "Yeah, and I used to have a hamster

named Burning Bush but he escaped. Our dog Cheyenne belongs to my brother Josh. Our orange cat Nugget belongs to my oldest sister Heather, and the black and white cat Pixie is too busy hunting mice to belong to anyone. The cockatiels—well, we took pity on them because the owners didn't want them anymore, so they don't really count as pets."

"Maybe you and your other sister Brittany can share this one?" Katy suggested.

"Maybe—but Brittany is more interested in driving her car than she is in feeding a cat!"

"If your parents won't let you keep the kitten, maybe my parents will let me have her," Katy said. "We don't have any pets."

When they reached the Anderson house, Robyn's mother was sitting at her desk talking on her business telephone. Cautiously, Robyn and Katy walked into her office. Mrs. Anderson's back was to them. A tiny "mew" caused her to swing around in her chair. With a look of surprise, she motioned to the kids to wait a minute while she finished her phone call.

"Yes, I'll give you a call as soon as I get that article written," she said to the person on the other end of the line. "It was great talking with you too! Bye!" She hung up the phone while staring at the frisky ball of fur that was nuzzling Robyn's arm. "I think that little thing is hungry," Mrs. Anderson said.

"Mom," Robyn began. "Before you say no, let me tell you how we found her." Robyn jabbered for 15 minutes, explaining how she had rescued the calico kitten from the "wild jungles of Blackbird Island."

"Wild jungles!" Mrs. Anderson exclaimed. "My, how fortunate for you that you weren't carried away by the island pirates. You know, the island is really called Blackbeard Island, after the famous pirate."

"Yeah, right!" Robyn said, laughing. "Well, maybe it wasn't a jungle, but there were sure a lot of tangled bushes and trees back in there."

"And I suppose you want to add this little critter to our growing zoo around here?" Mrs. Anderson asked.

Robyn could tell by her mother's amused look that the Anderson family was going to grow by one. She looked at Katy's disappointed face. "You can help me take care of her, if you want," Robyn offered.

Katy sighed. "Yeah, that would be fun. Maybe some-day I'll get a pet of my own. What are you going to name her?"

"Well, I've been thinking about that ever since I found her," Robyn said. Then looking quickly at her mother, she added, "That is, if you will let me keep her, of course."

"Of course!" Mrs. Anderson said.

"Well," Robyn continued, "I recently read C.S. Lewis' book, *Perelandra*. It's sort of a science fiction story based on the story of Adam and Eve. Perelandra is a lot like the Garden of Eden—full of beautiful trees and other plants. Since I found the kitten on a beautiful island, I thought I'd name her Perelandra."

Katy laughed. "Leave it up to you to give your pets unusual names—a hamster named Burning Bush and now a kitten named for the Garden of Eden!"

"I can't imagine how a kitten would end up on Blackbird Island," Mrs. Anderson remarked. Meanwhile, Perelandra found the food Mrs. Anderson had left out for their other cats and helped herself to every last morsel.

CHAPTER 5

Looking for Clues

When Mr. Jacobson arrived home from work, Johnnie presented the puppy to him and told him of the day's discoveries. Mr. Jacobson checked the little dog thoroughly—looking at his legs, ears, nose and teeth, and stroking his golden fur. Then he called the family together. "He looks healthy enough. And he is a golden retriever. Do we keep him?" Mr. Jacobson asked. "Everyone in favor, say yes."

Choruses of YES made it official—Steamer was part of the family. When everyone applauded, Steamer ran around the kitchen in circles, stopping for only a few seconds to wag his tail before he took off again. "Looks like he's pretty excited!" Mr. Jacobson remarked.

"I'm pretty excited too," Johnnie said. "I went tubing this afternoon to catch some waves—and I ended up catching a dog!"

The ringing of the telephone interrupted Johnnie's laughter. Mrs. Jacobson answered it. "It's for you, Johnnie," she said.

Johnnie wheeled himself over to where the phone was,

being careful to avoid Steamer who delighted in chasing Johnnie's wheelchair tires. "Hello?" he said. "Hi Danny! Guess what? Yep! I get to keep him. Cool, huh?" He talked with his friend for a few moments, said good-bye and hung up the phone.

"Dad, Danny is wondering if I could bring the wheelchair with the 'sand dune' tires to the dock this Tuesday. Mr. Randall said he would take us over to Blackbird Island that morning and pick us up later in the afternoon. We want to do some more exploring."

"Sure, I guess that would be all right. I'll have to transport the chair in our van as those tires aren't made for riding on pavement," Mr. Jacobson answered. "We'll put your regular chair in the van too so you can get yourself home again. Tell Mr. Randall that I'll pick up the dune chair that evening."

"Thanks, Dad!" Johnnie said. He picked up Steamer, who was whining and trying to jump into Johnnie's lap. "You're all right, boy. Let's go take a tour of the house."

Just then Johnnie felt something very warm in his lap. "Uh-oh," he said. "I think we should have started the tour in the backyard."

* * *

When Johnnie awoke on Tuesday, Steamer was cuddled beside him. "Time to get up, boy," Johnnie said. "I've got some exploring to do—and you get to stay home with Mom."

Steamer yawned, stretched out his legs and licked Johnnie's face. Johnnie scrunched up his nose and laughed.

After a quick breakfast, Mr. Jacobson called to his son from the driveway. "Come on, Johnnie! I've got your dune chair loaded in the van. Let's get you and the other chair inside."

Mrs. Jacobson picked up Steamer who was ready to follow his new friend out the front door. He wriggled around in her arms, trying to get loose. "Sorry, boy," she said. "You're not invited this time." Once Johnnie was inside the van, she put the pup down. He immediately ran to the front door and propped himself up against the screen, whimpering. "He'll be back later today," Mrs. Jacobson said. She walked into the kitchen and retrieved a puppy treat. "Come here, boy," she coaxed, kneeling down. She held out the treat.

Steamer's head turned toward Mrs. Jacobson, and in a few seconds, he bounded toward the kitchen and snatched the treat from her hand. Mrs. Jacobson smiled as she stroked his soft head. "Let's go outside," she said. "You can keep me company while I do some gardening."

* * *

By the time Johnnie, Danny, Katy, Travis and Robyn

piled into the Randalls' motorboat, it was nearly 10:30. The air was already heavy with moisture, and it promised to be another hot summer day. Mr. Randall attached a tow rope from the back of the big boat to the front of the smaller motorboat. In the smaller boat were all the food and drink supplies the kids would need plus Johnnie's dune chair, which was securely strapped in.

Mr. Randall carefully pulled away from the dock, making sure the smaller boat was following behind. There were only a few boats out on the lake, which made navigating to the island faster. "I'll set anchor near the shore," Mr. Randall said. "Then Danny, you and Travis take the motorboat and go to the island. Unload it and come back for your passengers. I'll be back around two o'clock to pick you up."

Before long, the kids were safely on Blackbird Island. The first thing they did was organize all the supplies and food. "Let's put the cooler in the shade," Danny said. "Even with all the ice we packed in it, I'm not sure it's going to stay cool in this hot weather."

Among the supplies were two small animal carriers Robyn had brought—just in case! "I'm sure there weren't any more animals on the island," Katy said. "When you found Perelandra, I went looking—hoping I'd find another kitten! I checked everywhere and found nothing."

"Yeah, I looked everywhere too," Travis said. "I didn't even see any chipmunks or ground squirrels. Just some noisy seagulls."

"Well, the whole idea is to go exploring," Robyn said. "No matter what we find, we can always use the carriers to transport our 'treasures!'"

"I agree," Johnnie said. "Let's get this exploration underway. Since I obviously can't get my wheelchair through all those trees and bushes, I'll go around the island on the beach. Who will go with me?"

"Travis, why don't you and I both go with him?" Danny said. "You've already hacked your way through most of the wooded area of the island. Besides, we might find more clues as to how these animals got here if we stick to the shoreline."

"Fine with me," Travis said. "Let's take one of those animal carriers with us."

"Okay, Katy and Robyn," Danny said. "You two explore the woods. Let's all meet back here at one o'clock. That will give us about two hours to cover this island. Then we can compare notes, eat lunch and wait for my dad to come get us."

"I think we should each take some bottled water with us," Robyn said.

"Good idea," Danny said. He opened the cooler and

took out five bottles of mineral water and handed one to each person. "We'll take the tan animal carrier and you guys can take the white one. Good luck!"

Katy ran off into the woods with Robyn following close behind. Danny watched them disappear into the shadows.

"I sure hope Katy won't be too disappointed if she doesn't find a kitten," he said. "That's all she's been talking about since our last visit here."

The three boys slowly began navigating around the island. The sandy soil had rocks, driftwood and other debris scattered on it, but for the most part, it was easy going. At times, the shoreline disappeared completely and Travis and Danny had to push Johnnie's chair through the long dune grass and over a small hill before connecting with more beach.

"We've been here for over an hour and we still haven't found anything," Travis said.

"I guess it would help if we knew what it was we were looking for," Danny answered.

"So far, I haven't seen anything out of the ordinary," Johnnie said. "I haven't heard anything out of the ordinary either."

"Look! Over there," Danny said, pointing toward an unusually flat and clean portion of beach. "The sand bar goes pretty far out into the lake. This would make a good landing place for a small boat. Maybe the next time we come here, we should come to this side of the island."

As the boys came closer to the beach, Johnnie leaned forward in his chair and squinted to see something close to the woods, about 25 feet from the beach. "Hey! I see something shiny over there," he said. "Let's go find out what it is."

Danny and Travis helped Johnnie push his way across the beach and toward the spot where the sunlight was reflecting off of something made of metal. "Hey!" Johnnie said, as they drew closer. "It's a dog dish."

Travis and Danny ran over to the dish. "It's got food in it!" Danny cried. "Looks something like dried puppy food—only it's a lot smaller."

"That's cat food!" Travis said. "We've got cats, and that looks a lot like what they eat."

"Should we bring this back with us?" Johnnie asked.

"No, I have a feeling we should leave it right where we found it," Danny said.

With the discovery of the container of pet food, the boys were anxious to get back to the meeting spot and tell the girls what they found. "We have 45 minutes to make it back," Johnnie said, glancing at his watch. "Let's keep watching for more clues but let's go as fast as we can."

The rest of the trip around the island took the full 45 minutes. The three boys were breathing hard by the time they arrived at the meeting place. There, waiting for them, were Katy and Robyn.

"Hey! Guess what we found!" Johnnie yelled as they trudged over the sand. "We found a dish full of dried cat food!"

"Really!?" Katy said. "And I'll bet I know why it was there."

As the boys drew nearer they could hear tiny scratching and mewing sounds coming from inside the animal carrier that Katy was holding.

"Another kitten?" Danny said, clearly surprised.

"No," Katy answered. "Two kittens!"

Danny, Travis and Johnnie watched in wonder as Katy carefully opened the little door. Robyn helped her retrieve the two tiny balls of fur. One was a medium gray with white markings. He was the bigger of the two. The second had similar markings but was black and white. Their eyes were a light olive green and seemed to be too big for their little heads.

"I don't believe it!" Travis said. "I know they weren't here before."

"We could have just not seen them," Robyn said. "We found these two curled up next to each other in a wild blackberry patch."

"We almost walked right by them, but then one of them mewed," Katy said. "They really didn't give us much trouble when we went to pick them up. I think they're both hungry though."

"Speaking of hungry, I know I'm starved," Travis said. "We've got about an hour left before Mr. Randall comes, so let's eat and rest."

"Did you say you found some cat food?" Katy asked.

"Yeah, but it took us 45 minutes to get to where we found it," Danny said.

"Yes, but you were traveling around the island pushing Johnnie," Katy reminded him. "I bet it would take a lot less time if we cut through the woods."

Katy and Robyn each grabbed a sandwich and a can of soda. "We've got these woods practically memorized. Watch my kittens. We'll be back soon," Katy said.

Within a half hour, Robyn and Katy were back with an empty sandwich bag filled with cat food. The boys were lying on the warm sand taking a nap. The kittens were also napping inside the animal carrier. Wisely, Danny had moved the carrier into the shade and had the front facing the breeze.

The girls dropped a few nuggets of food into the carrier but the kittens didn't seem interested. "I hope they'll be okay," Katy said. "I think I'll ask my parents if we can take them over to see the veterinarian Dr. Hamilton when we get home."

"Do you think your parents will let you keep two kittens?" Robyn asked.

"For sure!" she said. "I already asked them if I could keep any kitten we found on the island, and they said okay."

"Yeah, but they were talking about one kitten," Danny said, as he sat up from his nap.

"I'm only talking about one kitten," Katy answered. "One for me and one for you!"

"Hey! Works for me—I just hope it works for Mom and Dad," Danny said.

"Looks like you guys will find out pretty soon," Robyn said. "Here comes Mr. Randall."

CHAPTER 6

Stake Out!

"Can we keep them?" Katy yelled as her father anchored the boat a short distance from the island.

"Keep what?" Mr. Randall yelled back. The kids were still on the island gathering their things. Katy and Robyn gently removed the kittens from the animal carrier and held them up so Mr. Randall could see them. "Two kittens!" He was obviously surprised. He motioned for them to come out to his boat.

Katy, Robyn and Travis, along with the two kittens secured safely inside the animal carrier, scrambled aboard the small motorboat. Danny took the helm and transported them to the bigger boat. Once they were aboard, he went back for Johnnie, the supplies and Johnnie's chair.

After everyone was safely on board and the smaller motorboat in tow, Mr. Randall peered into the cage at the wide-eyed kittens. "They sure are cute," he admitted. "I'll have to check with your mother." Then noting the worried look on Katy's face he added, "I'm sure we'll be able to manage it somehow."

Katy jumped up and down with excitement and nearly fell overboard.

"Which one is going to be mine?" Danny asked.

"Well, I was thinking you could have the boy kitten and I'll take the girl," Katy replied.

"I was hoping you'd say that," Danny said. "Now, which is which?"

"The gray and white one is the boy," Katy said. "What are you going to name him?"

Danny looked inside the cage. His kitten was sitting up straight looking back at him. "He looks like a statue," Danny said. "I think I'll call him Oscar."

"Oscar?!" everyone said together.

"Hey! He's my cat," Danny said with a smile. "He looks like an Oscar. You know, like that famous award movie stars get."

"You could name yours Emmy," Mr. Randall said to Katy.

"Emmy?" Katy said, wrinkling her nose.

"Yeah, you know—it's the other award movie stars get. There are Oscars and Emmys," he said.

"That's a cute idea," said Robyn.

"Well, I think it's corny," said Katy. "I think I'll name her Minnie."

"Minnie!" Danny said. "Like in Minnie Mouse?" He

laughed at his own joke.

"No," Katy said. "Minnie—like in Minnie Randall, my little kitten. Yours looks like an Oscar and mine looks like a Minnie." She stared hard at Danny, daring him to make fun of her kitten's name. Danny got the message.

"Cool name!" he said. "I like it. Oscar and Minnie— sort of has a ring to it, you know!" Everyone laughed.

* * *

That evening it was official. The Randalls adopted Oscar and Minnie. Katy made them a bed out of some old blankets and a shallow cardboard box. She and her mother drove to the grocery store to buy kitty litter and food. Katy bought them catnip mice to play with.

"It's amazing that you kids found so many baby animals on that island," Mrs. Randall commented. "How do you suppose they got there?"

"I don't know," Katy said. "Maybe some people just wanted to get rid of them."

When Katy and her mother returned home, Danny was on the telephone talking to Johnnie. "Then it's settled," Danny said. "We'll camp out on the island tomorrow night. I have a tent that will easily hold you, me and Travis. If Katy and Robyn want to come, they can use the smaller tent."

"What are you guys talking about?" Katy asked.

"We want to stake out the island—see if anyone shows up with more animals," Danny said. "We'll bring our motorboat to that other beach we found—the one where we found the cat food. Travis and I can hide the boat, and then all of us can set up camp in the woods."

"Ugh! I don't think I want to camp out in the woods," Katy said. "But I'll call Robyn and see what she wants to do."

Robyn wasn't too crazy about the idea either. "Tell you what," she said, "let the guys do this campout thing and then they can tell us what happens in the morning."

"Sounds good to me," Katy said.

* * *

The boys set out for Blackbird Island about three o'clock the next day. Because they had camped out before, Johnnie's parents felt confident that Danny and Travis could help Johnnie with setting up his sleeping bag and transferring in and out of his wheelchair. With sandwiches, cookies, soda and chips packed, along with binoculars, flashlights and some board games, Mrs. Randall drove them to the dock.

Johnnie looked at all the camping gear, his dune wheelchair and the cooler full of food. "Definitely two trips," he muttered. "Hey Danny, why don't you load as much of this stuff into the boat as possible. Then you and Travis can take it to the island. I'll stand guard over the food until you come back for me." He smiled as he patted the cooler.

"I can stay here with you," Mrs. Randall offered.

"No, that's okay," Johnnie said. "As long as I'm near a food supply, I'll be fine. But thanks for offering."

She laughed and got back into the van. "All right, you guys! Have fun. I'll be back around ten tomorrow morning to pick you up."

Johnnie watched as she drove away. Travis and Danny had nearly loaded the motorboat. "I think we can fit that cooler in here," Danny said.

"Oh no you can't," Johnnie protested. "I'm holding it as ransom."

Travis and Danny smiled. "Well, okay," Danny said, "but just remember, I know exactly how much of everything is in there."

Before long, Danny and Travis took off to Blackbird Island. Johnnie watched as the boat appeared to get smaller and smaller. He glanced up at the sky. It had been a hot day but now gray, wispy clouds lightly blanketed the sky and helped block out some of the sun's rays. A gentle breeze fingered its way through Johnnie's dark-brown hair.

"Boy, I love a good mystery!" he said, smiling. "This is going to be awesome, I just know it." He sat with his eyes closed, thinking of the possibilities.

After what seemed to be just minutes, Johnnie heard the motorboat in the distance. Danny was coming back to get him. Soon they were on their way to an evening of adventure.

Travis had already set up the camp by the time Danny and Johnnie arrived. Travis helped Danny hide the boat, and soon the boys were busily talking and playing games. Around 8:30 it started to get dark.

"Looks like it's going to be a clear night," Johnnie said, noting that the wispy clouds had gone away.

"Yes, and it's supposed to be a full moon, so there will be plenty of light," Travis said.

"I wish we could have a campfire," Danny said, "but it would be too risky. If someone does come here tonight, I don't want them to know we're here."

Before long, the sun's golden crown sank beneath the horizon. The lights of boats on the lake twinkled in the distance as did the lights of the homes and stores that dotted the coastline. The gentle lapping of the waves on the shore made Johnnie sleepy. "I think I'll go lie down for awhile," Johnnie said. "I'm tired of sitting in this chair." He set the brake on the chair and inched his body forward. Travis and Danny helped him slide smoothly onto the carpet of leaves. Johnnie pulled himself into the tent and rolled onto his sleeping bag. The air was warm. Danny and Travis decided to join him inside the tent. From the front of the tent they had a clear view of the beach.

It hadn't been more than an hour before the distinct sound of a motorboat engine became louder and louder. Johnnie was the first to spot the boat's lights. "Someone's coming here!" Johnnie whispered.

Danny and Travis were instantly alert. The silvery light from the moon made it easy to see shapes and forms. The motorboat's silhouette came into full view as it approached the island.

The boys couldn't clearly see who was in the boat but they thought there was only one person. Suddenly, it became silent as the motorboat's engine was turned off. The person got out of the boat, carrying what looked like a big bag.

"It's a lady!" Johnnie whispered in surprise.

The boys hardly dared to breathe as they watched her come over to the dog dish and pour in what sounded like more food. "I sure hope you find this," she said. Unexpectedly, she looked toward the place where the boys were lying, holding their breath. She quickly grabbed the bag and ran back to where her motorboat was waiting. In a matter of seconds, the motorboat came alive as she maneuvered it back into deeper waters.

"Quick!" Danny yelled. "We've got to follow her."

Travis and Danny picked up Johnnie and ran to the place where their motorboat was hidden. They quickly helped him in and then shoved the boat into the water. Danny pushed the boat's throttle as far as it would go, making the little boat nearly leap right out of the water. "Hang on!" Danny shouted. "We can't let her get away!"

CHAPTER 7

Mystery Person

Water sprayed into Johnnie's face as he, Danny and Travis bounced over the waves trying to narrow the distance between them and the other motorboat. "It's no use!" Danny yelled. "She's too far ahead."

"Just keep your eye on where she docks her boat," Johnnie yelled back over the roar of the motor.

In a matter of minutes, the first motorboat's racing engine slowed to a purr as the woman eased the boat toward a wooden dock. The boys noted where it was and made a beeline toward it. By the time they pulled up on the other side of the dock, she was nowhere to be seen.

"Hurry, Travis," Danny said. "Let's tie up the boat. I'll help Johnnie out onto the dock while you run out toward the road. I'll catch up with you."

Johnnie used the strength he had to help hoist himself out of the boat and onto the dock. With Danny's help, it only took a few seconds. "Go!" Johnnie yelled. "I'll look around here for any clues."

Danny took off after Travis and soon disappeared

around the corner of a building. The light from the moon danced off the water and made the shoreline and trees look a silvery blue. Johnnie took advantage of the sky's "natural flashlight" to look for clues. He noted that the woman's motorboat had been hastily tied to the dock. "One good wave and that rope could come undone," Johnnie said to himself. He peered inside the boat from his position on the dock. "Hmm," he said. "Nothing unusual there. Just a lifejacket."

As he looked around the shoreline, the moon's light reflected off something small and shiny. Johnnie lay on his stomach and pulled himself toward the end of the dock. When he reached the sand, all he had to do was roll a few feet and he was right next to the small, flat object.

The sound of running feet caught Johnnie's attention, and he looked up. Danny, panting hard, called out, "Johnnie! Where are you?"

"Down here!" Johnnie answered. "Did you catch up with her?"

Travis and Danny sat beside Johnnie, trying to catch their breath. "We got to the street just in time to see her get into a car and drive off," Danny said.

"She looked like she was fumbling through her purse," Travis added. "If she hadn't stopped to look for her keys or whatever she was looking for, I doubt that we would have seen her at all."

"We weren't close enough to get a license number," Danny said. "I'm not even sure what kind of car she was driving. Once she heard us running toward her, she jumped in her car and took off."

Travis slammed his fist into the sand. "Nuts! If we had just come a few minutes earlier. Now we may never know who she is and what she was doing on Blackbird Island."

Johnnie, who had been busily examining the object he had found, suddenly said, "Don't be too sure about that."

Travis and Danny looked at him questioningly. Then Johnnie looked at them and smiled. "I'll bet Veronica Picazo was looking for this." He held up a leather wallet with a driver's license showing through the front plastic window.

Travis grabbed the wallet and looked at it, his mouth opened wide. "Where'd you find this?" he asked.

"I found it right here," Johnnie said, patting the ground beside him.

"Let me see that," Danny said. "Wow! It's got her address right here! Guess who will get a surprise visit tomorrow!"

"Let's get back to the island and think this through," Travis said.

"We can let the girls in on it tomorrow," Danny said.

"I think Nick is back from his Colorado vacation," Johnnie said, "and Joey gets back from camp tomorrow morning. We'll have to catch those two up on what's been happening!"

CHAPTER 8

Confrontation

After some quick telephone calls, the "Gun Lake Adventure Squad," as they liked to call themselves—including Nick and Joey—gathered over at Danny and Katy's. Johnnie explained to Nick and Joey what had happened so far. "It's a good thing you're back," he said to both of them. "I think something big is going on here, and we'll need your help to get to the bottom of it."

"How far away does this Veronica person live?" Joey asked. "We did a lot of hiking at camp, and I don't think I'm ready to hike anywhere too far yet."

"According to the city map my dad has, it's about three miles away," Travis said.

"Three miles!" Joey groaned. "I'll bet it's all up hill."

"Now, if you want to talk about hiking uphill," Nick said, "I'll talk to you about uphill. We must have hiked five miles straight up in the Rocky Mountains."

Robyn rolled her eyes. "Straight up?" she said.

"Well, it seemed like it was straight up," Nick said.

"I don't think we're going to have to worry about doing any mountain climbing around Gun Lake," Danny reminded them. "And who said anything about hiking?"

"Well, then," Katy said, "how are we going to get to Veronica's house?"

"We'll bike over there," Danny said.

"And what about Johnnie?" Robyn wanted to know.

"Oh, don't worry about me," Johnnie said with a smile. "I have an handcycle."

"A what?" Travis asked.

"It's like a bicycle," Johnnie said, "only it has pedals up by the handlebars. I steer and pedal at the same time. Did you know that some people with disabilities actually enter races using handcycles? And they go pretty fast."

"Cool!" said Nick. "Maybe if I get one, my legs won't get so tired."

"No, but your arms will," Johnnie said, and he laughed.

Travis paced back and forth shaking his head. "Can we just get on with this?" he said. "I've got to be back home by dinnertime."

"Travis, it's only ten in the morning," Katy said.

"My point exactly," Travis grumbled. "At the rate we're going, we won't even leave here until this afternoon."

"Okay, okay," Danny said. "Everybody go home and get your bicycles—or handcycle, and meet back here in a half an hour."

"Remember to bring your bottles of water and bike helmets," Katy said. She turned to Johnnie and added, "You do wear a bike helmet, don't you?"

"I sure do," Johnnie said. "When we were in California, a friend of mine was racing his dad down a long hill. My friend hit a patch of gravel, skidded sideways and flew off the bike. He landed right on his head."

"Oh, no!" Robyn gasped. "Did he get killed?"

"No," Johnnie replied. "He was lucky—and smart. He was wearing a helmet but he hit his head so hard that he damaged his spinal cord. Now he uses a handcycle because he can't use his legs anymore."

"You call that lucky?" Travis asked.

"I sure do," Johnnie replied. "The doctor said that if he hadn't been wearing a bike helmet, he would have likely died—or had severe brain damage."

"Wow!" Joey said. "For sure I'm wearing my helmet."

"Me too," Nick chimed in.

* * *

By 10:30 the next morning, the group was back at Danny and Katy's, ready to go. "What's the plan?" Robyn asked.

"If we travel the road that runs around the lake, we won't have any trouble finding Veronica's house," Travis answered. "We'll all wait in front of the house while Katy,

Robyn and maybe Nick go up to the front door with the wallet. Veronica has already seen Danny and me, and she might not open the door to us."

"Sounds like a good plan," Danny said. "Let's roll!"

The trip around Gun Lake took a little longer than the kids had anticipated. The air was thick with humidity and, even though it was still morning, the air temperature was nearly 85 degrees. Johnnie did well on his handcycle, but he tired quickly in the heat and had to slow down. By the time the kids arrived at the street where Veronica lived, everyone was sweaty and tired.

"Let's rest awhile and get cooled off," Robyn suggested. "I don't want to go up to Veronica's house looking like I just stepped through a sprinkler and nearly drowned."

"What time is it, anyway?" Johnnie asked.

"It's almost 11:30," Danny replied. "Let's rest about 15 minutes and then go to her house."

Fifteen minutes passed quickly, and though they were all breathing easier and had managed to cool off somewhat, their faces were still bright pink with the heat. "Well, it's now or never," Katy said. "Let's get going. Instead of just standing outside her house, why don't the rest of you wait at the end of the block? I'll wave at you if we need you."

Reluctantly, the boys agreed that the girls and Nick

would have a better chance of getting to see Veronica if they were out of sight. Katy, Robyn and Nick left their bicycles with the others and walked to about the middle of the block.

"Let's see, her address is 1845," Robyn said, as she examined Veronica's drivers license.

"That's the house, over there," Nick said, pointing to a small white house. Large sunflowers towered over the little white fence that ran along the side of the house. Brightly colored gladiolas bloomed on graceful, long stems. They bent slightly with the weight of the large flowers. A rose bush filled with scarlet, fragrant flowers climbed a trellis that leaned against the front of the house.

The inside front door was ajar but the screen door was securely shut. "Well, someone has to be home," Robyn commented. The palms of her hands were sweaty and she could feel her heart pounding.

Both Katy and Robyn hesitated at the bottom of the two steps that led up to the front door. With a sigh, Nick pushed his way between the two girls, jumped up to the small cement stoop and rang the doorbell. Katy and Robyn looked at each other but didn't make a move.

After a few seconds, a small, dark-haired woman came to the door. Her long, single braid hung heavily over one shoulder.

Katy grabbed the wallet out of Robyn's hands and bounded up the steps before Nick had a chance to say anything. "Hello, ma'am," Katy said. "We're here to see Veronica Picazo. Is she home?"

"No English," the woman said, shaking her head. She began to back away from the door.

"No! Wait a minute," Robyn said. "Don't go away. We want to speak with Veronica." Robyn's voice became loud and she pronounced each word slowly and carefully.

"Why are you yelling?" Katy asked. "Do you think she'll understand you better if you talk loudly?"

Robyn was about to answer when the woman said, "*¿Hablas español?*"

"Um," Robyn began to answer.

"That means, 'Do you speak Spanish?'" Nick interrupted. Then to the woman he said, "*Sí, hablo un poco español.*"

"You speak Spanish!?" Katy said. "I never knew that."

"My parents thought it would be a good idea to learn a second language, and so we've been taking lessons as a family," Nick replied.

"Amazing!" Katy said. "Well, ask her about Veronica."

In Spanish, Nick asked the woman if Veronica was home. The woman answered that she was at work. She said she was Veronica's mother and asked if she could help them.

"Should I tell her about the wallet?" Nick asked the girls.

"No," said Robyn. "Just ask her where Veronica works."

"*¿Dónde trabaja Verónica?*" Nick asked. He went on to explain that it was *muy importante* (very important) that they see her in person that day.

The woman hesitated and then said, "*Un momento,*" (one minute) and scuffled back into the house. A few moments later she came back with a small white business card. She opened the screen door and handed it to Nick.

Nick looked at the card. On it was Veronica's name, the name of the business she worked for, its address and telephone number. "*Gracias,*" Nick said. The woman smiled and waved goodbye as she stepped back into the house.

Nick, Robyn and Katy rejoined the others who were waiting at the end of the block. "Well?" Travis said. "What did you find out?"

"We found out that Veronica works for a place called Lakeside Shelter, and that it's at 4351 Sumner Street," Nick answered, holding out the business card.

Travis quickly unfolded the city map he had carried with him. Along the side were the names of the streets in alphabetical order. Beside each street name were letters and numbers. The map was divided into a grid. The lines on the grid that ran north and south were labeled by letters of the alphabet. The east and west lines were numbered. By intersecting the letter lines with the number lines, the kids could find the street on the map. Sumner Street had a G,5 next to it. The street they were on was labeled H,5. "We're not too far from where Veronica works," Travis announced. "Follow me!"

Travis led the group through several streets that were lined with small houses. At last they came to Sumner Street—a small dirt road that was sparsely dotted with small homes. At the end of the street sat a little brown, weather-worn shack. The numbers "4351" were painted in white letters on the front of the house, just over the black mailbox that hung at an angle near the front door.

"This is where Veronica works?" Katy said. "The lawn looks like it hasn't been mowed in a month!"

Danny rode down the street toward the house. "Look!" he yelled. "There's another larger, long building behind the house. It almost looks like an old barn."

The kids rode down the asphalt driveway that led to the barn. There was a small door on one end that was partially open. Johnnie pedaled his handcycle to the doorway. "I have some experience in barns," he said with a smile. "Let me take a peek."

He gently opened the door wider and gasped. The other kids quickly got off their bikes and scampered to look inside the barn. There, behind a small wooden desk, sat Veronica.

She heard the scuffling outside and looked up, obviously surprised to see seven pairs of eyes staring at her. She stood quickly and, with a frown, walked toward them.

"What do you want?" she said sharply. "What are you kids doing here?"

At first everyone was speechless. Then Johnnie held out Veronica's wallet. "I—we—thought you might want this back," he said.

Startled, she took the wallet and examined it. "Where on earth did you find this?" she asked.

"You dropped it last night—just after you came back from Blackbird Island," Danny said. "We were the ones who followed you from the island."

CHAPTER 9

Precious Cargo

Veronica's face paled and she looked as if she were going to faint. "So it was you who followed me," she said. "I was so scared. I was afraid you were my boss."

"Why would you be afraid of your boss?" Robyn asked.

"He's not a very nice man," she replied. "But I shouldn't be talking about him."

"Why do you work for a man who isn't very nice?" Katy asked, not willing to drop the subject.

"I need the money," Veronica said weakly. "My mother moved here from Mexico last spring when I graduated from high school. I was an exchange student, and after I graduated I decided to try finding a job here in the United States—to help pay for my college tuition. I am the youngest one in my family. My father died two years ago, and—well, my mother and I decided we should make Michigan our home—at least for now."

"We met your mother earlier today," Katy said.

"So she's the one who told you where I work," she said. "Which one of you speaks Spanish?"

Nick stepped forward and raised his hand. "I do," he said. "But just a little."

Just as she was about to say something else, the sound of a motor roared down the driveway. The vehicle screeched to a stop. Veronica's eyes widened and her hands began to shake. In a low voice she said, "You kids shouldn't be here. Thank you for returning my wallet but you really must go now."

Before any of the kids could turn around, a large, heavy man stomped through the open doorway. "What are you kids doing here?" he yelled. "If you're selling cookies or magazines or anything else, we don't want any!"

In a shaky voice, Nick began to say, "We just came here—"

But Danny caught the terrified look on Veronica's face and interrupted. "We were just on our way out." He placed his hand firmly on Nick's shoulder and turned him around toward the driveway. The others followed.

The man slammed the door shut. From the driveway, the kids could hear him yelling. While some of the words weren't clear, the few that the kids could make out were enough to make them hang around to hear more.

"What if he hurts her?" Joey said, his eyes wide with fright.

"We'll call the police," Danny said. "But it doesn't

sound like he's hitting her. I don't hear her screaming or anything."

"Shhhh," said Robyn. "I want to hear what he's yelling about."

The kids strained to make out the words. All they could understand was, "I told you to get that shipment out last night. . . .phone calls in the middle of the night . . .you will lose your job if . . .get busy NOW!"

The kids were heading back up the driveway when the man stormed out of the building and headed for his pick-up truck. He was so angry that he didn't even notice them. They scurried back to the street and turned toward the part that dead-ended. If the man was going to go any-where, he wouldn't turn that way.

Sure enough, the truck's tires burned rubber as he sped out of the driveway and zoomed down the street. "Gosh! I'll bet he's doing a hundred miles an hour!" Joey said. "Let's go home."

"We can't go home yet," Johnnie said. "We have to make sure Veronica's all right."

Danny said, "Katy and Robyn, why don't you stay here with Nick and Joey. Travis, Johnnie and I will go back and find out what's going on."

"S-s-sounds good to me," Joey said.

"I think I can get my bike through that front door,"

Johnnie said. "It would be better if we went inside—just in case Mr. Ugly comes back."

Travis and Danny agreed. They went back to the door and turned the knob. The man had slammed it shut so hard that it was difficult to open it right away. Travis put his shoulder to the door and gave a huge push. The door suddenly gave way, and Travis stumbled into the room, followed by Danny and Johnnie.

Veronica, who was sitting at her desk, screamed and jumped out of her chair. Her eyes were red from crying.

"What are you still doing here?" she screamed. "If he comes back and finds you here we'll all be in trouble."

"Don't worry," said Danny. "We watched him speed out of here. We also heard some of what he said."

Veronica was still trembling and trying hard to fight back tears. She collapsed in her chair and held her head in her hands.

"Are you all right?" Travis said. "Did he hit you or anything?"

"No, he didn't hurt me," Veronica said. "He sure scared me though."

"Well, what is going on?" Johnnie said. "I can't believe you are working for such a mean person. Isn't there any other job you can get?"

"I'm not a United States citizen," Veronica explained.

"At least, not yet. Finding a job when you're just a high school graduate—and from a foreign country—is not so easy. I need enough money to pay the rent and buy food, so I can't just take any job."

She looked as if she were about to cry again. But she pulled herself together and opened a desk drawer. She pulled out a file and began going through the papers. "I-I really have to get back to work. He may have sped off but he'll be back. I have to get the—the shipment ready."

"Shipment of what?" Danny asked. "Animals, maybe?"

Travis and Johnnie looked at their friend in surprise. Veronica's eyes widened and she opened her mouth as if to speak, but nothing came out.

"I'm right, aren't I? It has something to do with shipping animals," Danny said.

"I—I really can't talk about this. Please leave. I have to get this order ready. And he will be back. You don't want to be here when he returns. Believe me!"

Danny sighed. "Okay, we'll leave. But if there's anything we can do to help, please let us know. Do you have another business card?"

Veronica fumbled around in her desk drawer a few seconds and then pulled out a white card. "Here," she said, handing it to Danny.

Danny picked up a pen that was lying on Veronica's

desk and wrote his name and phone number on the card. He handed the card back. "You can get in touch with us through that number," he said. "I mean it. We can help."

Danny, Travis and Johnnie turned to leave. "Thank you," Veronica said. "Thank you for coming back."

By the time the boys met the others back on the road, Joey was near tears. "Can we go now?" he asked. "Please?"

Johnnie ruffled his hair. "Yep! We can go now. Danny gave Veronica his telephone number in case she wants to talk. She seemed pretty scared of her boss."

"Well, we have Veronica's telephone number too," Nick reminded them, holding out her business card.

"If she doesn't call us, then we'll call her," Johnnie said. "By the way," he said to Danny, "what made you think that this has to do with animals?"

"Well, she did come to the part of the island where we found the dog dishes," Danny said. "And I saw an animal cage sitting on the floor toward the back of her office."

"Hmm," Katy said. "Do you think she's the one who brought all those animals to Blackbird Island?"

"I have a hunch that she is," Danny answered. "And I am going to find out why—one way or another."

CHAPTER 10

Disappearing Pets

"You can't get the sock," Johnnie teased as Steamer yanked on his end of the sock with all his puppy strength. Little playful growls came from Steamer's throat as he tried to jerk and twist the sock out of his new master's hand. Just then the telephone rang and Johnnie let go, sending the surprised puppy rolling backward, the sock triumphantly hanging out of his mouth. He scampered off to the kitchen with his prize, looking back at Johnnie as if daring him to follow.

Laughing, Johnnie answered the phone. Danny was on the other end.

"Guess what?" Danny said. "Veronica called and said she wants to talk."

"Wow!" Johnnie said. "When? Where?"

"She said she could meet us during her lunch hour, so I suggested the Lakeside Ice Cream Shop. She said she could meet us at 11:30 this morning. Can you be there?"

"That should be okay," Johnnie said. "My mom and I were going to go shopping for school clothes but I can ask her to drop me off at the ice cream place when we're done."

* * *

When Johnnie arrived at their meeting place, Katy, Robyn, Danny and Joey were already there. Johnnie could see Nick riding his bicycle toward the small lakeside store. He looked around but didn't see any sign of Veronica.

"Hey, guys," Johnnie said as he wheeled himself into the store. Danny held the door open for him.

"Veronica said she'd be here by 11:30," Katy said. "What time is it, anyway? Maybe something happened to her. Maybe that horrible man she works for found out and wouldn't let her come. Maybe . . ."

"Gee, Katy, it's only 11:25!" Robyn interrupted. "Let's at least wait until she's late before we panic."

Katy stared hard at Robyn for a few seconds and then chuckled. "Okay," she said, folding her arms in front of her and staring up at the store's clock. "She has five more minutes and then I'm calling the police!"

Everyone laughed. Suddenly Travis stood up and pointed outside the front window. "Look! That's her car pulling up."

"I'll go out and meet her," Danny said. "She looks really scared."

The kids watched as Veronica parked her car and got out. She looked up and down the street, then quickly began walking toward the store. Danny was there to greet her. She looked relieved to see him but anxious to get inside.

The ice cream shop owner, Mr. Walker, had pushed two of his largest tables together for the kids. "We're having an important meeting in here," Travis had told him earlier. "We'll need chairs for seven people—oh, yeah— we'll also need an open space for Johnnie's wheelchair."

Mr. Walker had raised an eyebrow at Travis and said, "An important meeting, eh? It seems like the last time you kids had an important meeting here, you ended up getting involved in a mystery. Is this another one of those kinds of important meetings?"

Travis had smiled at Mr. Walker and answered, "You bet!"

Without further comment, the tables and chairs were set up. Mr. Walker hummed the "Mission Impossible" theme song as he worked. Travis just shook his head and laughed.

Now, he and the others sat at the table and waited for Veronica and Danny to come in and take their seats. When Veronica saw all the kids, she looked as if she were going to back out. But Danny encouraged her to come in.

After she had taken her seat, she and all the kids ordered lunch. Besides ice cream treats, Mr. Walker served hamburgers, hot dogs, chips and soda. The menu wasn't very big but the food was great—all the hamburgers and hot dogs were individually grilled.

After the waitress had left with their orders, Veronica looked down at her hands, which were tightly folded in her lap, and sighed. "I'm glad you agreed to meet with me," she began slowly. She lifted her head and looked at each of the kids. "Sometimes, it just isn't easy to do the right thing. I'm scared about what will happen to me and my mother if I lose this job—but I'm even more scared about what will happen if I don't stop what's going on."

Veronica hesitated a moment and looked as if she were going to cry. Katy scooted her chair closer to Veronica and looked up at her. "Don't be scared," she said. "We're your friends. If there's one thing we're really good at, it's helping our friends."

The others nodded in agreement and then waited for Veronica to start talking again. She smiled, her lower lip quivering a little and then said softly, "I don't have many friends—at least not in this country. When you came back yesterday, just to make sure I was okay after my boss had yelled at me—well, then I knew I really did have some friends. It gave me the courage to come here today, and I'm really glad I did."

Just then the waitress arrived with everyone's order.

Veronica waited until all were served and the waitress had left again before she began speaking.

"You have to understand," she said, "that when I took this job I thought I was going to be working with animals—helping them. Mr. Johnson, my boss, would bring in animals that he said other people didn't want. I was to put them in cages, write the date of when they came in and help take care of them. Sometimes, when I'd come back to work the next day, some of the animals were gone. Mr. Johnson just said he had found homes for them. I didn't suspect anything wrong—until…"

She stopped and bit her lip. "Go on," Katy urged. "You didn't suspect anything until…"

"…until some of the animals came in with collars on them and ID tags. Most of them were dogs, but there were a few cats too. When I started to call the phone numbers on the tags, Mr. Johnson stopped me. He said that these animals were pets that the owners didn't want anymore.

"I found that hard to believe. I mean, I'm such an animal lover that I couldn't imagine anyone just wanting to get rid of their pets. There was one beautiful golden retriever. She was just about to have babies. Mr. Johnson wanted me to keep a special eye on her because he said he had someone who wanted all the puppies.

"A few days later, I came back into work at night. There were some files that needed to be put away, and I just wanted to check on that golden retriever. Mr. Johnson was there, along with some other men. They were loading nearly all the cages into a big truck marked 'Professional Laboratories.' The golden retriever was left behind, along with some other animals—mostly cats. I heard one of the men say, 'We'll be back for all the puppies once they're weaned from their mother.'

"I had a feeling—a very bad feeling—about what I was seeing. I quickly left the building before anyone could see me. But before I left, I took down the information I saw on the truck. There was an 800 number written on one of the back doors. When I got home, I told my mother what I had seen. She agreed that I should investigate further.

"Well, to make a long story short, I found out that Professional Laboratories is a company in Connecticut that does research on animals. Now I know that animal research is necessary in order to test drugs that will later be used on humans but I didn't like the way these people were sneaking in at night and just taking animals that had once worn collars."

"So what did you do?" Robyn asked. "Did you confront Mr. Johnson?"

"Yes, as a matter of fact, I did," she replied. "He was

furious that I had been there. He accused me of spying. He said that his job was to round up animals and sell them to research laboratories.

"When I thought about those poor puppies about to be born, I felt sick. Within a couple days, the golden retriever had her puppies. There were only three that survived, though. I don't know what went wrong. Mr. Johnson was really angry. He started making arrangements to sell the three puppies—even before they were completely weaned from their mother. Fortunately, the research lab said they couldn't pick them up for another six to eight weeks.

"One day I had an idea. I would try to rescue some of the animals—including those three puppies. I purchased a small animal carrier and loaded it with a kitten that was going to be put to sleep and one of the puppies. I thought I'd tell my boss that one of the puppies had died and that I had buried it. I was afraid to take all three of them at the same time because I knew he would be suspicious."

"So you took the kitten and the puppy to Blackbird Island," Johnnie said.

Veronica looked surprised. "Well, yes I did. I had planned to take the other puppies too but when he found out that one was missing, he shipped the other two out before I could rescue them. I did find two more kittens, and I managed to take them out to the island. I put food out there and planned to go back every couple of days to check on them. But the last time I went I couldn't find any of them, and then I saw you kids. I got scared and left."

"Why did you take them to Blackbird Island?" Nick asked. "Why didn't you just let them loose in the country somewhere?"

"Because," Veronica answered, "Mr. Johnson goes looking for stray animals out in the country. If he finds someone's pet running loose—especially a gentle dog like that golden retriever—he just rounds them up in his truck and brings them back to his 'shelter.' I thought the animals would be safer on an island."

"Where did you get the boat?" Travis asked.

"I borrowed it from a friend of mine," Veronica explained. "I didn't tell him what I needed it for but he trusts me and said I could use it once in awhile."

Veronica looked out the window and sighed. "I sure hope those animals I put out on that island are okay."

"Oh, they're fine," Danny said. He smiled when Veronica looked at him questioningly. "Let's see, on our first trip to Blackbird Island, we found a golden retriever puppy—or actually, he found us! We also found a calico kitten. And then on our second trip, we found two more kittens."

Veronica let out a little gasp. "Are they all right?" she asked, in a hoarse whisper. She leaned forward and grabbed Danny's hands. "Are they all right?" she said louder.

"Yes! Yes! I told you they were fine," Danny answered. "We've adopted them. Johnnie has the puppy, Robyn has one of the kittens and Katy and I have the other two."

Danny thought Veronica would be relieved, but she looked even more worried. "Make sure you keep them in your house," she said. "Don't let them run loose. Mr. Johnson will be looking for them."

Robyn and Katy exchanged worried glances. Johnnie looked uneasy too.

"There must be something we can do to stop Mr. Johnson from stealing other people's pets," Travis said.

Just then Mr. Walker came up to the table. He knelt down between Veronica and Katy and looked at each kid sitting there. In a low voice he said, "I'm sorry that I over-heard parts of your conversation. But I must tell you that you all are going to need some help in solving this prob-lem. This Mr. Johnson sounds like a very greedy and un-feeling man—not the sort of person who will take kindly to people interfering with his business. You need some expert help. You need someone who really knows and understands the laws concerning the care and sheltering

CHAPTER 11

The Dog Law of 1919

That afternoon, Danny called Dr. Hamilton and asked if he and the kids plus Veronica could talk with him about "something really important."

"Well, I have appointments all day," he said. "Just how important is this? Is this for some fund-raiser for school or something?"

"Oh, no," Danny reassured him. "It's really important—like life or death kind of important."

"Oh my!" Dr. Hamilton exclaimed. "Well, should I cancel my appointments or do you think it can wait until five o'clock this afternoon?"

"I think it can wait until five o'clock," Danny said. "Thanks, Dr. Hamilton."

Danny quickly made the other telephone calls to Veronica and the kids. Veronica said she might be a few minutes late because she was supposed to work until five, and it would take her about ten minutes to reach the doctor's office.

"No problem," Danny said. "We'll wait for you."

of stray animals."

He stood slowly and gave Veronica and Katy a fatherly pat on the shoulder. "That's all I have to say. I don't want to tell you kids how to solve your mysteries—I just don't want anyone to get hurt." With that, he walked back toward his kitchen.

"He's right," Johnnie said. "We can't do this on our own. I wouldn't even know where to begin. But I know we have to do something. The idea that he might come and steal back Steamer scares me."

"Dr. Hamilton!" Robyn nearly shouted. "Dr. Hamilton, our veterinarian will know what to do. Let's ask him."

Veronica abruptly stood. "I—I must get back. Maybe I've done a terrible thing. I'll lose my job for sure and then what will happen to me and my mother?"

Johnnie wheeled his chair over to her and took her hand. "Veronica, believe me, I'm not an expert on where to find jobs. But I do know that when you have friends you can do anything."

The afternoon seemed to drag by. Johnnie spent most of it playing with Steamer and worrying about his newfound friend's safety. "I can't believe that you almost ended up as a laboratory specimen," he said, hugging Steamer's neck. The puppy just looked up at Johnnie and wagged his tail.

Katy and Robyn were also stunned by the news of what had almost happened to their kittens. "I can't imagine anyone being so heartless," Katy told her brother.

"Me neither," Danny agreed. "And I hope Dr. Hamilton can do something about it."

At 4:45 p.m. Johnnie met the other kids at the end of his block. Together they made their way to Dr. Hamilton's office, which was located in a small brick building that was narrow but long. When they opened the door, a little buzzer sounded somewhere in the back. The receptionist was nowhere to be seen so the kids took seats in the waiting room.

The walls were painted a light green and the floor was a soft white linoleum with little flecks of blue, green and gold in it. Hung along the walls were either pictures of various breeds of dogs, birds and cats or posters talking about different diseases that were treatable or preventable with proper care. In one corner there was a display of scientifically formulated dog and cat food. Just above it was a bulletin board covered with small photographs of and information about animals. They were apparently placed there by some of the owners of Dr. Hamilton's patients. Magazines were strewn on a low, square table set in the middle of the room. Johnnie wheeled over and picked one up. On the cover was a picture of a golden retriever.

He started looking through the magazine when a door leading to the back opened and a white-haired woman poked her head out. "You kids here to see Dr. Hamilton?" she asked.

"Yes," Danny answered. "I called and set up an appointment with him for five o'clock today."

"Well, he's just finishing up in back," she said. "Just make yourselves at home. He won't be but a minute." She gently closed the door and left the kids by themselves.

About ten minutes later Veronica came into the office. Again, the buzzer sounded in the back, telling the doctor and his receptionist that someone had either come in or gone out.

"Been here long?" she asked the kids.

"Just a few minutes," Johnnie said.

They heard the door in the back open again and the gray-haired woman poked her head out and looked around the room. "Heard the buzzer," she explained. "Just making sure you're still here." Then spying Veronica she said,

"Looks like we've added someone. Are you waiting with these other folks?"

Veronica smiled. "Yes, I am," she said.

"Well, it shouldn't be much longer now," she reassured them and disappeared behind the door again.

Veronica walked over to the bulletin board. Suddenly, she gasped and pulled a picture of a black cocker spaniel off the board.

"What's wrong?" Robyn asked.

"This dog," Veronica said. "Mr. Johnson brought a dog that looks just like this into the shelter yesterday. It had on a collar, but Mr. Johnson took it off and threw it in the trash."

"Maybe it's the same dog," Johnnie said.

"There's a note under where the picture was tacked up," Veronica said. "It says, 'REWARD offered. Family's pet lost August 15 in Gun Lake area. Black cocker spaniel answers to the name of Silky.'"

"That dog belongs to the Peterson family." Everyone jumped at the sound of Dr. Hamilton's voice. "Have you seen her?" he asked.

"N-no—well, that is, I'm not sure," Veronica said as she tacked the picture back onto the bulletin board.

"Silky is a beautiful dog. She's been in the Peterson family for about ten years now. They usually keep her inside their chain-link fence yard. I guess one day someone forgot to securely latch the gate and off she went," Dr. Hamilton said. "She does have a collar on her that gives her name, and ID number and a phone number to call, so hopefully someone will find her and give the Lighthouse Foundation a call."

"The Lighthouse Foundation?" Johnnie asked. "What's that?"

"It's a highly respected animal shelter," he answered. "They take in stray animals and try to find either the owners or other families to adopt them. They also raise money to pay for the animals to be spayed or neutered, treated for fleas and given their shots. For a small fee, people can have information about their pets entered into a computer system. Each owner answers a questionnaire about the pet. They give the animal's name, breed, age and a brief medical history—including whether the animal is spayed or neutered and when the last shots were given. Then the owner fills in his own name, address and telephone number. The animal is given a tag to wear on its collar. If it gets lost, someone who finds it can call the telephone number listed, which is Lighthouse Foundation's special animal-tracking number. By telling the Foundation what the ID number is, the Foundation can immediately track where it lives and contact the owner."

"Why don't they just have the owner's telephone number on it?" Joey asked.

"Partly for safety reasons," Dr. Hamilton said. "The Foundation arranges for the owner to either pick up the animal at the person's home who found it or arranges for the person to bring the animal to the Foundation, where the owner can claim it. That way, strangers aren't coming to the owner's house. Another reason is that every time an animal is lost and found, the Foundation notes that in the animal's record. Sometimes animals get away from their owners and head to the same part of town. If an animal is found in an area once, chances are it could be there again.

"But anyway, I'm sure you didn't come to hear all that. What's this 'life and death' situation you were telling me about?"

Danny looked at Veronica. "I think you'd better tell him the whole story," he said.

Veronica looked uneasily at Dr. Hamilton and hesitated. He looked steadily into her eyes and gave her a warm smile. Grabbing the chair that sat empty behind the receptionist's desk, he placed it next to an empty chair in the waiting room and sat. He indicated that she was to sit in the chair next to him. She did so, but slowly.

"Veronica, you can trust Dr. Hamilton," Danny said. "He's our friend, and you're our friend, so I guess that makes him your friend too. Right, Dr. Hamilton?"

"Absolutely!" he said. He leaned toward Veronica slightly and said, "Now why don't you just tell me whatever it is that's bothering you."

Veronica took a deep breath. "Okay," she said. "Here goes."

After about a half an hour, she finished telling Dr. Hamilton everything. He leaned back in his chair, a frown on his face. "Veronica, this is very serious business you're talking about," he said. "The law is very specific about animal research. Most of the time, animals are bred and raised just for that purpose. But when people start stealing pets—that's a whole different story.

"Tell me," he continued, "how are the animals treated while they are at the shelter where you work?"

Veronica shifted uncomfortably in her seat. "We—I mean Mr. Johnson—has metal cages for them to stay in. I've seen as many as six or seven full-grown cats crammed into one cage. Same for puppies and kittens. There's usually one bowl for water and one for food per cage. Except for that one golden retriever, he didn't have me work much in the back. I would sign them in and then sign them out whenever he told me they were gone."

"You were looking at that picture of Silky. Do you think you've seen that dog in your shelter?" Dr. Hamilton asked.

"I'm not sure it's the same one," she answered. "Maybe I can go back tonight and look through the trash for that collar he threw away."

"Yes, I think that would be an excellent idea—as long as that won't put you in any kind of danger," the doctor said.

"As far as I know, Mr. Johnson won't be at the shelter tonight. I overheard him say that the next research truck was due this Saturday—just two days from now," she answered.

Dr. Hamilton rose from his chair and walked to the receptionist's desk. He opened a drawer and pulled out a small 35mm camera. He looked at the back of it. "Hmm, looks as if it has about 15 pictures left on this roll of film." He handed the camera to Veronica. "If you think you can do it, I want you to take this camera and get pictures of the animals that are kept in that shelter. Find that collar and any records of the animals that are currently there. If that truck is coming on Saturday, we haven't much time to lose."

"Why can't we just call the police and have them raid the place?" Nick asked.

"It's not that easy," Dr. Hamilton said. "There are laws—one in particular is called the 'Dog Law of 1919.' It talks about how animals are to be cared for whether they are at home or in a shelter. There needs to be plenty of food and water. The place where they stay needs to be kept clean. There needs to be shelter where they can go if the weather outside is bad. If they are in a shelter, wherever they are kept needs to be sanitary, and the animals must be able to get some exercise. Also, if there are stray dogs with tags on them, the law says they must be held a minimum of one week to give owners a chance to find them. If they don't have tags, shelters can get rid of them after four days."

"Get rid of them?" Nick yelled. "What do you mean 'get rid of them'?"

"They can euthanize them—put them to sleep," Dr. Hamilton answered gently.

"Put them to sleep?" Nick's voice rose to a high pitch. "You mean kill them, don't you? Why do animal shelters kill the animals they are supposed to be trying to help?" he demanded.

Dr. Hamilton knelt down in front of Nick and took him gently by the shoulders. He looked directly into Nick's eyes and said quietly, "Nick, I know that putting animals to sleep is something neither one of us likes. But sometimes it is necessary. There are so many animals without homes that shelters simply can't care for them all. Many shelters, like Lighthouse Foundation, do everything they can to find adoptive homes. But if shelters become filled, then other stray animals can't come in."

Nick's eyes filled with tears. "It's just not fair," he moaned.

"That is why it is so important to have your pets spayed or neutered," Dr. Hamilton said.

"What is 'spayed' or 'neutered'?" Joey asked.

"It's a simple surgical procedure that simply means boy cats won't become fathers and girl cats won't become mothers," Dr. Hamilton explained.

"But kittens and puppies are so cute," Katy said. "Like the kittens we got from Blackbird Island."

"Yes, they are cute," Dr. Hamilton admitted. "But for every cute kitten that is adopted there are many that are not. Those that are not adopted often die terrible deaths. We certainly don't want that to happen, do we?"

Nick slowly shook his head, as did the others.

"But, in the meantime, we have to see if we can help rescue the animals that are at that shelter Mr. Johnson runs," Dr. Hamilton said. "We have to have evidence that shows the law has been broken."

"What if Silky is at that shelter?" Johnnie said. "If Mr. Johnson decides to put Silky in with all those other animals that are going to the lab on Saturday, won't that be breaking the law? I mean, Silky wouldn't have been there a whole week."

Dr. Hamilton's face lit up. "I think you're on to something there, Johnnie." To Veronica he said, "Just get me those pictures and that collar—and any records you can find."

Danny said, "Let's go and help her. Some of us can keep a lookout, just in case Mr. Johnson decides to come back, and the rest of us can look through trash bins for that collar."

"It will look better if I don't go with you, at this point," Dr. Hamilton said. "Call me at home as soon as you find out anything. We'll go down to the police station with the evidence it will take to stop Mr. Johnson."

Johnnie noticed the frightened look on Veronica's face. "Don't worry," he said. "You'll see. Everything will work out."

CHAPTER 12

Finding the Evidence

It was 7:00 p.m. when Johnnie situated himself on the seat of his handcycle. He waved goodbye to his parents and headed off to meet the rest of his friends. His heart rate quickened, not just because he was pedaling fast but because he was thinking about his previous encounter with Mr. Johnson.

"I sure hope that man finds something to keep him busy and away from the shelter tonight," he muttered under his breath. Within a few minutes, he arrived at the meeting place.

"Okay, who wants what job once we get to the shelter?" Danny asked, once everyone had arrived.

"Well, I for one want to stay near the trees as a lookout," Nick said.

"Me too!" Joey chimed in.

"What about you, Johnnie?" Travis asked. "What do you think you can do? I mean with that long handcycle thing of yours, isn't it going to be a little tough to go riding around in that small building? And what if that Mr.

Johnson decides to make an appearance? How will you get out of there?"

"Well, since I got in there once before and didn't have too much trouble moving around, I figure I can do it again," Johnnie replied. "Besides, I thought I could go in the back and take the pictures. If Mr. Johnson comes back, I'll think of something. There's got to be a back door somewhere. What about you Travis? What do you think you're going to do?"

Travis shrugged. "I don't know. I'm not one for looking through trash bins. And I doubt Veronica will need my help looking for records. I guess I'll just hang with Nick and Joey and keep them out of trouble."

"I'll help Johnnie take pictures," Danny said. "We've never been in the back room before. Who knows what we'll find there?"

"Well, I guess that leaves you and me to look for that dog collar," Robyn said to Katy.

"There's nothing gross in the trash bins, is there?" Katy asked. "I mean, are we going to have to put our hands into anything gushy?"

"I hope not!" Robyn said.

"Wait a minute," Travis said. "What if this Johnson guy *does* come zooming down the street in his truck? What are Joey, Nick and I supposed to do about it?"

"Hmm," said Robyn. "He does drive awfully fast. If we're in the middle of a trash search, I don't know how much time we would have to get out of there."

"We've got to slow him down somehow," Travis said.

"Hey! I have an idea," Nick said. "Why don't we pull out one of those big dead tree branches from the woods? We could put it across the road so he'd have to stop to get it out of the way."

"That's a great idea!" Johnnie said. "If Joey is up by the tree branch, just looking like he's playing or something, then as soon as he sees the truck coming, he could wave at Nick, who would be at the end of the block. Nick could then give the signal to Travis who could run in and tell us!"

"Sounds like a good plan," agreed Danny. "I think we'd better get going if we're going to meet Veronica on time."

The kids pedaled hard and arrived at the shelter out of breath. Veronica's car was parked in the driveway. Travis, Joey and Nick searched for and found a large oak tree branch. It was so large that it took the three of them plus Danny to move it up the street.

"Let's put it up at the beginning of the block," Travis said, "just before it curves. That way, he'll have to get out of the truck but won't be able to see the shelter. Joey, you'll be just beyond the curve so you can see both the truck and Nick. That way you can give him the signal and not be seen by Mr. Johnson."

"I hope no one else has to use this road," Danny remarked. "Then they would move the branch and Mr. Johnson could sail on through!"

With the branch in place, Joey, Nick and Travis took their places, and the rest of the kids went inside the shelter. Veronica was busily looking through files. She looked up when the kids came inside.

"Hi!" she said. "I just got here a few minutes ago."

"Danny and I are going in the back to take pictures," Johnnie said. "Do you have the camera Dr. Hamilton gave you?"

She handed them the camera. "There are about five cages of animals back there," she said. "And one of the animals is that black cocker spaniel we were wondering about."

"Okay, while the boys go take pictures, Katy and I will look through the trash bins. Where are they?" Robyn asked.

"They're outside behind the building," Veronica answered.

"Is there anything—well, you know—gross in those trash bins?" Katy asked, wrinkling her nose.

Veronica laughed. "Not really. It's mostly paper. And the trash service hasn't emptied the bins yet, so I'm sure that collar is in there somewhere."

Robyn and Katy looked at each other and shrugged. "Oh well," Katy said, "I guess we'd better hurry up and get this over with." They went outside and walked around to the back of the building.

Johnnie and Danny slipped into the back room. "Ugh!" Johnnie said. "This place smells bad."

"It smells like these cages haven't ever been cleaned," Danny agreed.

As they looked around, they found five cages of animals, just as Veronica had told them. They weren't prepared to see the filth and the crammed quarters the animals had to live in. Some of them didn't even have room to lie down properly. In the back corner was the cage that held the cocker spaniel and one other dog. Other cages were filled with kittens and puppies. Some of them had infections in their eyes. Flies buzzed mercilessly around the cages.

"Look at this water dish!" Johnnie exclaimed, pointing into one of the cages. "It's practically empty, and it looks dirty."

Danny looked around for a water bucket or hose. "I can at least give them some water," Danny said.

"No! Wait a minute," Johnnie said. "Let's get the pictures first."

The boys carefully photographed the animals and the conditions in which they had to live.

Meanwhile, Robyn and Katy were frantically sorting through paper in the first of two trash bins. "I hope we get lucky," Katy said. "Going through someone else's trash gives me the creeps."

"Me too," Robyn agreed.

Just then Katy felt her hand scrape against something that was thicker than paper. It felt stiff, about an inch wide and long. "I think I may have found the collar!" she yelled.

She quickly pulled it out from under all the paper, and there it was. A long blue collar with the tags in place. "Look!" she cried as Robyn stood beside her. "It's got an ID number and a telephone number on it. And look at this," she said pointing. "It's got the name 'Silky' written on it."

"Bingo!" Robyn said. "Now we'd better hurry and put all this trash back."

Just then the phone inside rang. Veronica jumped when she heard it but decided not to answer it. The answering machine picked it up. Mr. Johnson's gruff voice said, "The shelter is closed. Leave a message and we'll get back to you." Then there was a long BEEP.

"Hey Johnson," the voice on the other end said. "Where are you? You said you'd be there at eight o'clock. Well, anyway, me and my partner will be there on Saturday at four o'clock to pick up those cages. See you then." Click.

Veronica looked at her watch. It was eight o'clock, and apparently Mr. Johnson was supposed to be there. "Oh no!" she said. "We'd better get out of here."

Just then she heard the familiar roar of a truck engine coming down the street. Joey heard it too and looked up to see Mr. Johnson speeding toward the tree branch. Frantically, Joey signaled Nick, who had also heard the truck.

When Mr. Johnson saw the tree branch, he slammed on the brakes and the truck screeched to a stop. "What the—!" he yelled. He swung open the truck door and tugged angrily at the branch.

Meanwhile, Travis had picked up the signal and warned everyone to get out of the building. Katy and Robyn threw the last piece of paper in the trash. Danny, determined to give the dogs some water, ran the hose over to the water dish while Johnnie turned on the water. It sloshed into the dish, spilling some on the floor. Veronica ran in the back and handed Danny the papers she had found. "Get out of here!" she said. "Go out the back. I'll stay here and finish putting food and water in the dishes. Then he won't be suspicious of why I'm here."

The kids ran out the back, collected their bicycles and blended into the nearby woods. Joey, Nick and Travis were already headed into the wooded area by the dead-end when Mr. Johnson's truck roared up to the shelter's front door. The kids waited, wondering if Veronica would be safe. A few minutes later she came out and slid into the drivers seat of her car. She looked scared but unharmed. After she drove away, Mr. Johnson came out and got into his truck. He sped away up the street.

"Whew!" Johnnie said. "That was close! Let's get out of here and call Dr. Hamilton."

By the time the kids arrived back at Danny's house it was nearly nine o'clock. Danny picked up the phone and punched in Dr. Hamilton's home phone number. When the doctor answered, Danny quickly told him what they had found.

"Do you have that camera?" Dr. Hamilton asked.

"Yep! Got it right here," Danny answered. We took all 15 pictures—including a couple of Silky."

"Are you sure that dog is Silky?" Dr. Hamilton asked.

"According to the dog collar we found, it is," Danny said.

"Great!" the doctor said. "Meet me at my office at nine o'clock tomorrow morning, and be sure to bring the camera and anything else you have. Contact Veronica and ask her to come too."

CHAPTER 13

A Surprise for Veronica

The next morning, Dr. Hamilton took the film to a one-hour film developer. Veronica was there, as well. While they waited, he looked over the records Veronica had found. Basically they were dates that new animals were brought in and dates when they left. Payment records were also included in the stack of papers, including the name of the laboratory to which the animals were sold.

Just as the film was ready, the kids hurried into the store. When Dr. Hamilton pulled out the pictures his face grew grim. "Disgusting!" he said. "Absolutely horrible."

"What? What?" Nick wanted to know.

He showed them the pictures, then turned to Johnnie and said, "You and Danny certainly captured the absolutely terrible living conditions these poor animals have had to endure. I can't believe anyone would be so heartless and cruel. This alone will give us reason to go to the police, and I've already alerted Chief Davis that you kids are on to something."

"Then what are we waiting for?" Johnnie said. "Let's

go!"

When they arrived at the police station, Chief Davis wasn't there. "I told him we would be stopping by," Dr. Hamilton said to the sergeant at the desk. "There's an illegal shipment of animals due to leave a shelter that is in clear violation of the law at four o'clock this afternoon, and we have to stop it."

"Sorry," the sergeant said, "Chief Davis stepped out of the office. But I think he'll be back around noon. Is there something I can do in the meantime?"

Dr. Hamilton showed the officer the pictures, Silky's dog collar and some of the records. "We know that Professional Laboratories is going to pick up all the animals you see here. Some of them have been there for about four days—which is the required time they need to be held if they don't have a tag. Well, we know for sure that Silky was brought into the shelter only two days ago, and she had a tag on—and she's going to be shipped out with the rest of the animals this afternoon. I also happen to know that this dog belongs to Mr. and Mrs. Peterson, and they have been looking everywhere for her."

"Well, we're going to have to get a judge to issue a search warrant, and that might be hard to do on a Saturday afternoon," the sergeant said. "Why don't you folks stop back here around noon when the chief gets back? In the meantime, I'll check around and find out what judges are in town."

Disappointed, the kids, Veronica and Dr. Hamilton left the police station. It was 10:45 a.m.

"An hour and fifteen minutes!" Danny said. "I don't know if I can wait that long."

"I think I should call the Petersons," Dr. Hamilton said. "They should be able to positively identify their dog, in case Mr. Johnson starts denying everything. In the meantime, why don't we all go over to the ice cream shop for a hamburger and milkshake? My treat!"

Mr. Walker's special burgers and shakes helped the time go by quickly. At noon, the troop marched back into the police station. The sergeant looked up and smiled. "Chief Davis just came back a few minutes ago, and I filled him in on what you told me. He said to have you go back to his office." He pointed to several small offices in the back of the building.

Just as they started down the hallway, Chief Davis came out of his office to greet them. "Hi there kids! Hello Dr. Hamilton." He stopped when he spotted Veronica.

"This is Veronica Picazo," Dr. Hamilton explained. "She and her mother are new here, and Ms. Picazo works at the animal shelter in question."

"Oh!" the chief said. "Well, I'm very happy to meet

you." Then he turned to the doctor and said, "Let's see what you have here."

Dr. Hamilton gave the police chief the pictures, collar and records. "I hear that a truck is coming to pick up these animals at four o'clock," Chief Davis said. "Is that right?"

"Yes sir," Veronica answered. "That's what the man said on the answering machine."

"Well, that doesn't leave us much time. But Sergeant Gray found out that Judge Hackley is in town, so I think our first order of business is to get a search warrant issued."

After Chief Davis located the judge, getting the search warrant took about two hours. It was 2:30 p.m. and time to confront Mr. Johnson. "I don't think it would be a good idea for all you kids to go out there," Chief Davis said. "There might be trouble."

Katy and Robyn looked down at the floor and tried to hide their disappointment. Danny and Travis just looked at each other, their mouths open. Nick and Joey didn't know what to do, so they just inched toward the door, ready to leave. But Johnnie spoke up.

"We're the ones who uncovered all of this," he said. "I don't mean to be disrespectful, Chief Davis, but we were the ones who risked our very lives to dig up all this evidence. Couldn't we at least go in someone's van and watch from the road?"

"Risked your very lives, eh?" Chief Davis said with a smile. "Well, I don't know about that."

"I have a van at home, and I would be happy to take responsibility for our young detectives," Dr. Hamilton offered. "What about Veronica and the Petersons?"

The police chief rubbed his chin thoughtfully. "Well, I can certainly see why you would want to be there, and if Dr. Hamilton will bring you in his van and keep you at a safe distance from the shelter, I suppose it will be okay with me."

The kids began smiling and making promises to be good when the chief interrupted, "But, you will all have to get written permission from your parents to be in that van and to accompany me to a potential crime scene."

When the kids began to protest that it would take too much time, Dr. Hamilton intervened. "Look," he said. "Why don't each of you call your parents and have them meet us here in a half hour, if they can. I'll explain the whole thing to all of them and find out if they will let you come."

"What if they say no?" Joey asked.

"If they say no, then it's no," Dr. Hamilton said. "We can't go against the wishes of your parents."

One by one the kids made their phone calls. Fortunately, one parent from each family was home and able to come down to the police station. By three o'clock, the parents were all assembled.

"What have you kids gotten into now?" Johnnie's dad asked.

"Well, you should be proud of them," Dr. Hamilton said. And he went on to explain the whole story.

"Is this going to be dangerous?" Joey's mom asked.

"There are no guarantees," Chief Davis said. Then when he noticed the worried looks on some of the parents' faces he quickly added, "But Dr. Hamilton has assured me that he will keep the children in the van and at a safe distance away. I will have three more police officers with me, so I think the risks are minimal."

"Should we go along?" Danny's father asked.

"I'm already stretching it in having the van full of kids come," Chief Davis said. "But I suppose if you want to come in another vehicle or two and park next to the van, that would be okay."

In short order an agreement was arranged. All the parents wanted to be there, and so Mr. Jacobson and Mr. Randall agreed to drive the parents. The clock on the wall showed that it was 3:30 p.m.

"We'd better roll if we're going to beat that truck," Chief

Davis said. By this time the Petersons had arrived. They and Veronica were to ride in the back of Chief Davis' squad car. "Remember, this is only a search. I can't guarantee we'll find anything," he said.

The ride out to the shelter didn't take very long. To everyone's surprise, the long truck from Professional Labs was already there. Chief Davis and his fellow officers headed toward the front door. They were met at the door by Mr. Johnson.

"What are you doing here?" Mr. Johnson demanded. "What's going on?" Then he spied Veronica in the back seat of the squad car. "Just what did she tell you?"

Without answering his questions, Chief Davis handed Mr. Johnson the search warrant. "Please step aside," he said. He motioned for Veronica and the Petersons to join him.

As they stepped out of the car, Mr. Johnson suddenly ran back into the building and disappeared into the back room. Chief Davis and the others quickly followed him. As they entered the room, the last of the cages was being hurriedly carried out the back door.

"Put down that cage," the chief ordered.

The two men who were carrying it looked at Mr. Johnson to find out what he wanted them to do.

"Drop the cage," he growled.

"No!" Chief Davis said. "I said to put the cage down—gently."

The two men obeyed. Inside were six small kittens, mewing miserably.

The other officers hurried out back to discover another man closing up the back of the truck.

"Hold it right there, mister," one of the officers said.

"You don't have a warrant to search my truck," one of the men said.

"We have a warrant to search this building and anything on the premises," the officer replied. "This truck is on the premises so step aside."

The officers opened the door. Inside were four cages filled with animals. The Petersons ran outside. Mr. Peterson climbed into the back of the truck. There, in the far right corner, was the cage that contained the black cocker spaniel.

"Silky!" Mr. Peterson yelled.

At the sound of his voice, the dog began to wag its tail and whimper. Silky scratched at the door and tried to get out.

Mr. Peterson quickly undid the latch and let out his beloved pet. The dog looked a little thin but seemed all right.

By this time, Johnnie, the other kids and their parents

had gotten out of the cars and stood watching and listening. Several residents stood outside their homes too.

"You're under arrest," Chief Davis said to an angry Mr. Johnson.

"For what?" Mr. Johnson snarled.

"For cruelty to animals, not providing them with a clean and properly maintained shelter and for illegally getting rid of animals that were properly tagged, for starters," the chief answered calmly. Over Mr. Johnson's protests, Chief Davis read him his rights, handcuffed him and then helped him get into the back seat of one of the squad cars.

"What's going to happen to this shelter?" Johnnie yelled out.

The chief turned and walked toward Johnnie. "If Mr. Johnson is found guilty, this shelter will be shut down," Chief Davis said. "There is a lot of evidence against him, and we have the testimony of Veronica here."

She looked hesitant but then said, "Yes, I will do what is right."

"What about the animals?" Joey asked. "The Petersons have their dog back but what about all these other animals?"

Dr. Hamilton put his hand on Joey's shoulder. "Don't you worry about a thing. I want all these animals taken back to my office. I will clean them, feed them and give them examinations. I'll contact the Lighthouse Foundation and let them know what has happened. We will make every effort to either find the owners or find new homes for these little creatures."

Then he looked at Veronica. "And I am going to need some help. How about it, Veronica, would you like to have a new job?"

Her face lit up and with a big smile she said, "Yes! Oh, yes! I would be so very happy to work for you!" All the kids cheered, and she gave everyone a hug.

"Let's get these animals back to their new temporary home," Dr. Hamilton said. "Veronica and I will work to get them cleaned and fed—and then I think we should all meet at Lakeside Ice Cream Shop for a celebration!"

As they were about to leave, Veronica walked over to Johnnie and knelt beside his wheelchair. "You know, you were right," she said softly. "When you have friends, you can do anything."

A portion of the proceeds from sales of The Gun Lake Adventure Series goes to support the nonprofit organization Alternatives in Motion, founded by Johnnie Tuitel in 1995. The mission of Alternatives in Motion is to provide wheelchairs to individuals who do not qualify for other assistance and who could not obtain such equipment without finacial aid.

For further information or to make donations, please contact Johnnie Tuitel at:

Alternatives in Motion

1916 Breton Rd. S.E.

Grand Rapids, MI 49506

(616) 493-2620 (voice)

(616) 493-2621 (fax)

Alternatives in Motion is a nonprofit 501(c)(3)
organization.

Gun Lake Adventures Series

Available titles:

The Barn at Gun Lake

Mystery Explosion!

Discovery on Blackbird Island

"Both vibrant, active stories (**The Barn at Gun Lake, Mystery Explosion!**)...feature great reading adventures with a memorable wheelchair bound hero who surprises his friends (and perhaps even himself) with what he can do."

- Midwest Book Review

"An excellent venture."

- WE Magazine

"One of the most unlikely groups of detectives ever conceived... in the book **The Barn at Gun Lake.**"

- The Grand Rapids Press

"**The Barn at Gun Lake** has what it takes to engage middle level readers..."

- Pooh's Corner Bookstore

"This little book is a gem."

- Early On Michigan Newsletter

Gun Lake Adventure Series

by Johnnie Tuitel and Sharon Lamson.

The Barn at Gun Lake (1998, Cedar Tree Publishing, $5.99 paperback, **Book 1**)
The Gun Lake kids stumble upon a cadre of modern pirates when they find an illegal copy of a popular CD in a deserted barn. While solving the mystery, there is a boat chase and then a harrowing wheelchair chase through the woods. This story is great reading adventure.

Mystery Explosion! (1999, Cedar Tree Publishing, $5.99 paperback, **Book 2**)
First there is an explosion. Then an arrest is made that shocks the quiet town of Gun Lake. A stranger in town, and a search for his identity, paves the way for another fast-paced mystery. Friendships and loyalties are tested as Johnnie Jacobson and the kids try to find the answers to "Who did it?" and "Why?"

For more information or distribution contact:
Tap Shoe Productions
888 302-7463 www.tapshoe.com